DREAMWORKS

MR. PEABODY & SHERMAN

Sherman's Awesome Adventures

DREAMWORKS

MR. PEABODY & SHERMAN

Sherman's
Awesome Adventures

Adapted by Molly McGuire Woods
Illustrated by Fabio Laguna

Random House New York

Chapter 1

My name is Sherman. I am seven years old, and I live with my dad. Sounds pretty normal, right? That's because you haven't met my dad. His name is Mr. Peabody. And he's a dog.

Mr. Peabody is also a genius. He flies around the world performing scientific experiments and meeting important people. The best part is that I get to go with him!

Mr. Peabody adopted me when I was a baby. It didn't make sense to some people. Why would a dog genius want to raise a human baby?

It made perfect sense to Mr. Peabody. Sure, he had done a lot in his life. But he always said that something—or someone—was missing.

That someone was me! I feel proud that Mr. Peabody chose *me* as his son.

Being raised by a world-traveling genius has its perks—like the WABAC, for example. The WABAC is a totally awesome, top-secret time machine. Mr. Peabody invented the WABAC so we could tour history together.

"There's nothing like learning history first-hand," he always says.

Mr. Peabody and I travel through time and space, visiting all of history's super-cool moments. We ice-skated with woolly mammoths. We ate at the first Thanksgiving with the Pilgrims. We took part in the French Revolution. We make a great team. Mr. Peabody likes to teach me things, and I love to learn.

Sometimes, though, we run into trouble on our trips. Let's just say that an encounter with George Washington, an ancient Egyptian

wedding, and a gigantic black hole almost ruined my life.

It all started on my first day of school. Mr. Peabody drove me to school in our motorcycle and sidecar. He had plenty of last-minute instructions for me on the way. It was like he wasn't sure I could handle things on my own.

When we got there, I leapt out of the sidecar. "Bye!"

"Wait!" Mr. Peabody cried. He handed me a small silver gadget.

"Thanks," I said. I turned it over in my palm. "What is it?"

"It's a dog whistle," he replied.

I blew hard into the thin whistle. I didn't hear anything. "It doesn't work," I announced.

Mr. Peabody rubbed his ears. "It works fine, Sherman," he said. "But only *dogs* can hear it."

"Oh," I said with a shrug. "Cool!" I shoved it

into my pocket and walked toward the school.

Behind me, Mr. Peabody shouted, "No matter what challenges you face, no matter how far away I seem, I am always here for you."

"Bye!" I called again. Mr. Peabody sure had the first-day dad jitters. He wasn't used to me being on my own.

But I was excited to start school. With all my time travels, I felt ready—especially for history class.

• • •

"Who is George Washington?" my teacher asked the class.

I waved my hand in the air.

A girl with long blond hair raised her hand quickly, too.

"Sherman?" The teacher called on me.

"The first president of the United States," I answered.

"Good job," the teacher said, nodding.

I grinned. I tried to ignore the blond girl scowling a few desks away.

"When President Washington was a boy, what kind of tree did he cut down?" the teacher continued.

Again, the girl's hand shot up at the same

time as mine. The teacher called on her.

"Penny Peterson?"

"A cherry tree," Penny said.

"That story's not true!" I declared. Then I explained that George Washington never cut down a cherry tree. He also never said he couldn't tell a lie. "People made up those stories to teach kids a lesson about lying."

I could tell that my classmates—especially Penny—didn't believe me. "Washington did cross the Delaware River in 1776," I continued. "My dad took me there over the summer. We crossed the river, too. I almost fell in!"

My class laughed. They didn't know it, but thanks to the WABAC, I had *actually* been there in 1776. I'd also actually fallen into the river. I'm pretty clumsy sometimes.

"Well, it looks like someone knows their history," my teacher noted.

Penny crossed her arms and frowned. I didn't care if she believed me. I knew the truth.

. . .

I forgot all about Penny—until lunchtime. She came over to my table.

"What have you got there, Sherman?" Penny said, eyeing my lunch. "Kibbles or bits?"

"Actually, I've got carrots, juice, and a tuna sandwich," I replied.

"So you eat human food, then?" she asked.

"Yeah, why wouldn't I?" I retorted. What was Penny getting at?

"Because you're a dog," she sneered.

"No, I'm not," I said.

"Sure you are. Your dad's a dog, so you're a dog, too. Here, I'll show you." She knocked my sandwich across the lunchroom with her hand. "Fetch!" she ordered.

Everyone in the cafeteria gasped. I wasn't

sure what to do. None of Mr. Peabody's lessons had covered this.

"Go on, doggy, get your lunch," Penny teased. The crowd laughed.

"Sherman, get your food. Good doggy," Penny continued.

I took a deep breath. I asked myself what Mr. Peabody would do. He probably wouldn't care about everyone staring. But I did. Maybe if I just picked up the sandwich, Penny would stop. I bent over to get it.

"What's this?" Penny asked.

I spun around. My heart sank. Mr. Peabody's dog whistle dangled from Penny's finger. She must have swiped it from my pocket.

"What is it? A whistle?" she asked. She blew into it. "Doesn't even work."

"Give it back," I said. I tried to grab it from her hand.

"Jump, doggy! Jump!" she teased. She held it over my head.

I started to lose my cool. I leapt toward Penny. But she caught me in a headlock.

"Admit it! You're a dog!" she commanded.

"Let me go!" I ordered through clenched teeth.

"Not until you beg like a dog!" replied Penny.

The kids chanted, "Fight! Fight!"

There was only one thing to do. If she wanted a dog, I'd show her a dog.

I opened my mouth wide. . . .

Chapter 2

"I'm sorry I bit her," I said as Mr. Peabody tucked me in that night. "I won't do it again."

"You're darn tooting you won't do it again," Mr. Peabody replied. After the lunchroom fight, the principal called Mr. Peabody into a meeting. A woman from the Bureau of Child Safety and Protection was there. Her name was Miss Grunion. Mr. Peabody said we were in big trouble. Penny's parents wanted to file a complaint. Miss Grunion was even coming to our house to investigate.

"It's just not like you," Mr. Peabody said. "What happened?"

"She called me a dog," I whispered. I didn't

want to hurt his feelings. After all, being a dog wasn't a bad thing. But Penny sure had made it seem that way.

Suddenly, Mr. Peabody didn't seem mad anymore. "Thank you for telling me. Try to get some sleep."

"I love you, Mr. Peabody," I called.

"I have a deep regard for you as well,

Sherman," he said, closing the door as he left.

I tossed and turned all night. What would happen if Penny's family filed a complaint? Would I still be allowed to live with Mr. Peabody?

All of our adventures swirled through my head. One stupid fight couldn't ruin all that, could it?

• • •

The next afternoon, I found Mr. Peabody cooking a feast in the kitchen.

"Wow!" I exclaimed. "Is today a special occasion?"

"You could say," Mr. Peabody answered.

I tried to figure out what made today special. "It's not my birthday," I started.

"No," said Mr. Peabody.

"It's not *your* birthday," I said.

"Right again," he replied.

"Is the president coming again?"

"No," said Mr. Peabody.

I was stumped.

Just then, the doorbell rang. Mr. Peabody hurried to answer it.

I trailed behind him. "So who's coming to dinner?" I pressed.

"Let's just say that if this evening is a success, we can put this biting business behind us," Mr. Peabody replied. He threw open the door.

My jaw dropped in shock. Three people stood in our doorway. One of them had blond hair— and a bad attitude.

"The Petersons!" Peabody announced.

As in *Penny* Peterson and her parents. Why on earth would Mr. Peabody invite *them* to dinner?

"We're delighted you could make it," Mr. Peabody said, bowing. "Aren't we, Sherman?"

"Yeah," I mumbled. "We're interested in what's going on, for sure."

Mr. Peabody ignored my comment. "Say hello to Penny, Sherman."

I couldn't believe this. Not only was my worst enemy standing in my own hallway, now Mr. Peabody expected me to *talk* to her. "Hi, Penny," I grumbled.

Penny didn't look happy, either. "Hello, Sherman," she muttered. She clutched her bandaged arm.

"Why don't you go show Penny your mineral collection, Sherman?" Mr. Peabody suggested.

Dragging my feet, I led Penny to my room. What was Mr. Peabody thinking inviting the Petersons for dinner? Maybe he hoped they wouldn't file a complaint if they got to know us. All I knew was that no matter how fancy the dinner, Penny and I would never be friends.

After what seemed like forever, Mr. Peabody checked on us. "What are we supposed to do in here, anyway? She hates me," I whispered.

"Just make it work," Mr. Peabody murmured. "But don't tell her about the WABAC!"

I closed the door and turned toward Penny.

"Don't even think about it," she said, fuming.

"You know, Penny," I said, "Sigmund Freud says if you don't like a person, it's because they remind you of something you don't like about yourself."

Penny glared at me. "What do *you* know about Sigmund Freud?" she asked.

"More than you think," I replied. Mr. Peabody and I had visited the famous psychologist in the WABAC.

"Just like you know all about George Washington. What a crock!" Penny said.

"But it's true!" I exclaimed.

"How do you know?" Penny demanded.

"I just know!" I said.

"Did you read it in a book?" she asked, annoyed.

"No," I said.

"Did your brainiac dad tell you?"

"No," I replied.

"So how do you *know*, Sherman?" she said, poking me in the ribs. "How do you *know*?"

I couldn't take the pressure anymore. "He told me!" I blurted out.

Penny looked suspicious. "*Who* told you?"

"George Washington," I said.

"Liar." Penny rolled her eyes.

I was *not* a liar. So to prove it, I told Penny the one thing Mr. Peabody asked me not to. I should have known it would only make things worse.

Chapter 3

"He calls it the WABAC," I explained, leading Penny to the time machine.

I knew the WABAC was supposed to be a secret. But Penny had called me a liar. So I *had* to show her the time machine!

"Can the WABAC go back to an hour ago?" Penny asked me.

"Why?"

"Because I could take it home, pretend to be sick, and not come to this lame party," she replied.

"Ha, ha. Mr. Peabody says you should never use the WABAC to travel to a time when you existed."

"How come?" Penny asked.

"Because then there'd be two of you," I explained.

Penny nodded. "I guess the world's not ready for that."

I punched in a security code on the keypad and a door opened. **Whoosh**.

"Wow!" Penny said when she saw the machine.

My stomach tied itself in knots. Suddenly, this seemed like a *very* bad idea. What if Mr. Peabody found out? What if Penny told someone else? I was losing my nerve. "Now that you've seen it, maybe we should go back," I suggested.

Penny brushed me aside. "Are you kidding? Where should we go first?"

"Mr. Peabody says I'm not allowed to drive it," I said.

"Do you do everything that Mr. Peabody says?"

"Yes," I mumbled. Since when was following your dad's rules a bad thing?

Penny smirked. "You know what that makes you, Sherman? A dog."

I couldn't let her get away with that twice. I revved up the time machine. Next stop: 1776.

• • •

A short while later, I parked the WABAC at home—without Penny. Things had gotten out of control. Now I was safe, but Penny was still in the distant past!

I tried not to panic. All I needed was a plan. If I could rescue Penny before her parents knew she was missing, then no one would get hurt. But how? I snuck inside to find Mr. Peabody. He would know what to do.

"*Pssst.* Mr. Peabody? Can I talk to you?"

I whispered into the living room, where Mr. Peabody was busy entertaining the Petersons.

"Where's Penny?" he asked, crossing the floor to meet me.

I bit my lip. "Ancient Egypt."

Peabody's eyes bulged. *"You used the WABAC?"* he whispered. "How could you?"

I hung my head. "She called me a liar," I began. But when I said it out loud, it didn't seem like such a big deal.

"So you took her back in time?" Mr. Peabody asked.

"She was into it," I said.

Just then, the Petersons peeked around the corner.

"Where's Penny?" Mr. Peterson asked.

"Uhhh . . . ," I uttered dumbly.

"What's going on?" Mrs. Peterson asked.

I felt sick to my stomach.

"It's hard to say," Mr. Peabody replied. Then, to buy us some time, he waved his hands back and forth and hypnotized the Petersons into a trance.

I stared at their stiff, angry faces. I didn't want to see how they would look if we didn't bring Penny back from ancient Egypt.

"To the WABAC!" Mr. Peabody ordered.

Chapter 4

Seconds later, Mr. Peabody parked the WABAC in the hot desert of ancient Egypt. We walked toward a royal palace in the distance.

"No telling what kind of perilous position we'll find Penny in," Mr. Peabody said.

I gulped. I hoped Penny was okay. It would be my fault if she wasn't.

• • •

Inside the palace, we saw Penny sitting on a fancy chair. She wore a fancy dress. Egyptian servants fed her grapes. To think I'd been worried about her!

"Hi, Penny," I said.

"What are *you* doing here?" she asked.

Mr. Peabody cleared his throat sternly. "We are here to take you home."

"I'm not Penny anymore," Penny replied, walking with her nose in the air. "I'm Princess Hatsheput—precious flower of the Nile."

Mr. Peabody clutched her arm. "If you think we are going to leave you . . ."

"Unhand her!" a voice called. A boy dressed in fancy robes and jewels entered the room.

"Who's that?" I whispered.

"That is King Tut," said Mr. Peabody.

"He's my boyfriend," Penny said proudly.

Boyfriend? I could feel my eyes bulging out of my head. I sized up the king's skirt and makeup. Time travel had clearly messed with Penny's brain!

Just then, the royal astronomer, Ay, stepped forward. "The wedding must take place tomorrow," he declared.

Wedding? Were they for real?

Thankfully, Mr. Peabody stepped in. "Penny," he began, "the king dies young. Are you sure you've thought this through?"

Penny crossed her arms.

"Ay," Peabody continued, still looking at Penny, "would you tell the princess what it means to marry King Tut?"

Ay nodded. "It means she will be bound to him in eternity through mummification."

"Hold up," Penny said, confused. "Can someone walk me through that?"

King Tut explained. "It means that when I die, they'll kill you, too."

Penny's face turned white.

"Let the wedding preparations begin!" King Tut announced.

The royal servants picked up Penny and carried her away.

"Mr. Peabody! Sherman!" she cried helplessly.

"Don't worry, Penny! We'll save you!" I said. It seemed like the right thing to say. But that was before Penny's royal servants locked Mr. Peabody and me in a cold, dark pyramid.

• • •

"You can't just leave us here!" I shouted. "Mr. Peabody, can I hold your hand?" I found my dad's hand and gripped it tight.

"Sherman. That's not *my* hand," Mr. Peabody replied.

I looked down and saw I was holding the hand of a mummy. **"Arghhhh!"** I shrieked. This place gave me the creeps.

"Now to find a way out of here," Mr. Peabody said.

Even in the dark, I noticed stone coffins all around us.

"Look," Mr. Peabody said. "These tombs are lined with hieroglyphics. Maybe they will help us."

I squinted at the squiggly writing and symbols carved into the walls. They looked like a bunch of nonsense to me.

Mr. Peabody studied the hieroglyphics. "Hummmm," he muttered. "This one shows the god Anubis sailing the boats of Ra to the underworld. It appears the boats of Ra are the key to our escape! Then we must find Penny in time to stop the wedding."

"If you ask me, we should *let* her marry that guy. They deserve each other," I mumbled.

"Sherman, I'd say you are jealous," Peabody said, casting a sideways glance at me.

"You think I *like* Penny? Gimme a break!" I cried.

Mr. Peabody felt his way along the wall.

"Aha!" he cried, pulling a hidden lever. A secret passageway opened before us.

"Careful," Mr. Peabody warned. "One step in the wrong direction and we're done for."

I looked down at a pathway of rocks that zigzagged across the room. Each rock had a secret code carved into it.

Mr. Peabody carefully moved from one rock to the next. He decoded each message as he went. "The boat . . . of Ra . . . sails straight today. . . . Take the wrong boat . . . man will pay." He reached the other side of the room safely. He waved to me. "All right, Sherman, your turn. Do the puzzle exactly as I did."

I gulped. These types of puzzles were easy for Mr. Peabody. But not for me. I took a deep breath and launched myself forward.

"The—boat—of—Ra—sails—straight— today. . . ." I paused. "Take—the—wrong— boat—man—will—play. . . ."

Mr. Peabody winced.

"I mean **pay**!" I shouted, realizing my mistake. But it was too late. The tiles beneath me crumbled.

"**RUN!**" Mr. Peabody commanded.

We burst though a doorway just as the floor gave way beneath us.

• • •

The next thing I knew, we'd entered a huge cave. Two golden battleships floated before us.

"The boats of Ra!" Mr. Peabody exclaimed. "One boat is the way out; the other will send us plunging to certain death."

"Which boat is the *not*-certain-death boat?" I asked.

"That one!" he shouted, pointing.

They looked the same to me. I hopped onto

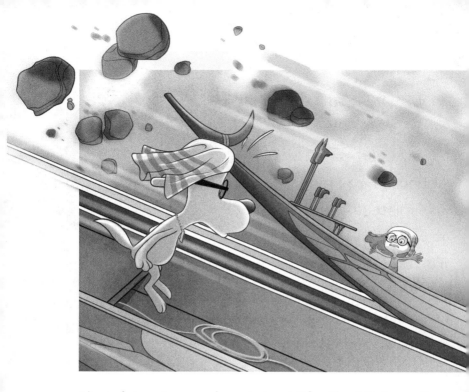

the closest one. I watched Mr. Peabody pull a lever on the wall and dive onto one of the boats. There was only one problem: we didn't choose the same boat! If Mr. Peabody was on the right boat, then *mine* meant certain death!

"What should I do?" I yelled. Rocks fell from the ceiling. My boat picked up speed. It headed toward a huge waterfall. I was going to die!

Quickly, Mr. Peabody tied a rope around his waist. He leapt onto my boat and grabbed me. We swung back to safety just as my boat tipped over the waterfall.

Chapter 5

We escaped our pyramid prison in Mr. Peabody's boat. Then we raced across the desert. We had to stop Penny's wedding before it was too late!

We saw Penny and King Tut standing before a large crowd. We hid behind a giant statue of Anubis, the god of death. He looked like an Egyptian man with the head of a dog.

"How are we going to get past all those Egyptian soldiers?" I asked.

"We need to trick them," Mr. Peabody whispered. Then he explained his plan. We would pretend to be Anubis and convince King Tut to call off the wedding. King Tut would be so terrified, he'd set Penny free!

As the wedding began, we climbed into the statue's oversized head. Mr. Peabody pulled out a megaphone.

"I am Anubis!" he said. "If this marriage pact is sealed, I will shower down upon the land uncontrollable plagues!" He was so loud, it really did seem like the statue was speaking.

While Mr. Peabody talked, my job was to make the Anubis statue look angry by blowing smoke around his face. We lit a fire. I fanned the smoke. It swirled around the statue's eyes and out the mouth.

The crowd looked terrified. So did King Tut. Our plan was working!

"Take the girl to the city gates and leave her," Mr. Peabody instructed.

The guards grabbed Penny. Suddenly, some ash from the fire fell on my foot. "Ow!" I cried, coughing from the smoke.

I tried to stamp out the ash with my foot. Then I heard a loud **craaack**.

The mouth of the statue broke and tumbled to the ground—taking us with it! The crowd was furious to learn that we had tried to trick them.

Thinking fast, Mr. Peabody jumped onto the broken mouth of the statue.

Penny and I hopped on behind him. We rode that mouth like a sled through the crowd and across the desert.

"Stop them, you fools!" Ay commanded.

We scrambled into the WABAC as spears whizzed past us.

We shot into the sky just in time.

All we had to do now was return Penny to her parents. Then life could get back to normal.

But then we heard an alert coming from the dashboard. **Beeeep!**

Mr. Peabody peered at the screen. "All that zipping about the cosmos has drained our power supply," he said. "We're going to have to make an unscheduled stop."

I groaned. How could we run out of gas at a time like this?

"We have just enough power to make it to the Renaissance and my old friend Leonardo da Vinci!" Peabody said cheerfully.

We were going to the 1500s.

• • •

We landed in Renaissance Italy and walked toward Leonardo da Vinci's house. Mr. Peabody explained that Mr. da Vinci was an inventor, a scientist, an engineer, and a painter.

"Peabody, old friend! What do you need?" Mr. da Vinci exclaimed.

"The WABAC needs a jump start," replied Mr. Peabody.

While they worked on fixing the WABAC, Penny and I explored.

We climbed into the attic of Mr. da Vinci's dark workshop. It was filled with crazy models and inventions.

"It's like a toy store!" said Penny.

One of Mr. da Vinci's flying machines sat in the corner. It looked like a boat with wings. Penny knocked on it to test its strength.

"Penny, we should leave that alone," I warned.

She climbed into the cockpit anyway. "Just tell me how it works," she said.

I explained how it was built.

"But how does it take off?" she asked.

"Oh," I replied. "You just pull down on that lever."

Penny yanked the lever toward her. The machine rocketed toward the window.

"**Ahhhhhh!**" I screamed, hanging on to the side for dear life.

"**Wooooo-hooooo!**" shouted Penny.

We shot out of the house. I struggled to climb into the cockpit next to Penny.

"We're going to die!" I cried.

Penny rolled her eyes. "Oh, stop being such

a party pooper. Here, Sherman, you fly it!" She tried to get me to take the steering wheel.

I shook my head.

Penny let go of the steering wheel. I felt the plane start to nosedive.

"You're going to have to save us!" Penny called as we fell through the air.

"But I can't!" I cried. "I'm serious. I don't know how to fly!"

"You can do it!" Penny replied.

I watched the ground get closer. It was now or never. I grabbed the steering wheel and pulled up. I felt the flying machine right itself.

"See?" Penny said. "You got this."

I grinned. Penny was right—I was *flying*! If only Mr. Peabody could see me. Maybe he'd even let me drive the WABAC!

Penny and I glided past Mr. da Vinci and Mr. Peabody.

"Sherman? **SHERMAN!** What are you doing?" Mr. Peabody yelled.

"I'm flying!" I called back.

"But, Sherman, you don't know how to fly!" Mr. Peabody shouted.

I panicked. Mr. Peabody was right. I *didn't* know how to fly. My hands started shaking. I lost control of the flying machine.

"**Ahhhhhh!**" I screamed.

"Turn, Sherman!" Mr. Peabody called.

It was too late. We crashed into a tree. Penny and I climbed down. We weren't hurt, but I couldn't say the same for the flying machine.

I should have felt bad for smashing Mr. da Vinci's invention. But instead I felt alive!

"That was pretty fantastic!" I called to Penny.

She just laughed.

Maybe we would be friends after all.

Mr. Peabody and Mr. da Vinci raced over.

"My flying machine works!" Mr. da Vinci cried.
"Sherman, you are the first flying man! You
should be very proud, Peabody!"

The look on Mr. Peabody's face told me that
he wasn't proud at all.

Chapter 6

With the WABAC running again, we were on our way home once more.

Mr. Peabody was not happy, though. "You could have been killed!" he scolded me.

"He was amazing!" Penny said.

"Miss Peterson," replied Mr. Peabody sternly, "stop turning my son into a hooligan. I've spent the last seven years teaching Sherman good judgment."

Penny crossed her arms. "If you're such a great parent, why is Miss Grunion trying to take Sherman away from you?"

My stomach sank. "Is that true?" I whispered.

Mr. Peabody frowned. "No, Sherman," he said. "I'll never let that happen. You just need to trust me."

Suddenly, we felt the WABAC swerve. Mr. Peabody tried to get control, but he couldn't. We barreled right toward a black hole!

"**Ahhhhhh!**" Penny cried.

The WABAC was sucked into the center of the most powerful gravitational field in the universe—like a coin down a drain!

Mr. Peabody looked worried. "If I can't pull us out of here, we are going to be smashed to smithereens!"

I was worried, but not about the black hole. I might not get to live with Mr. Peabody anymore—and he hadn't even mentioned it! Maybe we weren't the perfect team after all.

"Why didn't you tell me?" I shouted over the rattling WABAC engine.

"We'll discuss it later, Sherman. Sit!" Mr. Peabody commanded.

"You can't talk to me like that!" I cried angrily. "I'm not a dog!"

Mr. Peabody looked hurt. "You're right, Sherman. You're just a very bad boy!"

I felt a tear slide down my cheek. Mr. Peabody had never spoken like that to me before.

The WABAC crash-landed. I squeezed my way out and ran. I'd show them what life without Sherman was really like!

I heard footsteps nearby. I hid as an troop of Greek soldiers marched by. I recognized their uniforms from a book Mr. Peabody had shown me. Maybe they needed an extra man. . . .

• • •

A short while later, I adjusted my helmet and stood at attention. I tried not to think about Mr. Peabody. I was a Greek soldier now.

We lined up inside a giant wooden horse. We were going to use it to storm the gates of the city of Troy.

Our leader, Agamemnon, walked among the rows of soldiers. He stopped in front of me.

"Ready to get on the field, Shermanus?" he asked.

"Sure thing!" I felt like one of the team. I even had a nickname already!

We heard a knock outside.

"Shhh!" Agamemnon commanded. He opened the door and found a small wooden horse outside. He brought it in, and Mr. Peabody and Penny popped out!

"I've come to take Sherman home," announced Mr. Peabody.

I crossed my arms in anger. "Sorry, Mr. Peabody. I've joined the Greek Army," I told him, puffing out my chest.

Agamemnon nodded. "Shermanus is one of us now. Today he will prove himself on the field of battle."

"Sherman," Mr. Peabody said. "I'm concerned that you haven't thought this through. This is war. Do you realize what's about to happen?"

I hadn't actually given it any thought.

"I'll tell you what's going to happen!" Agamemnon shouted. "We're going to make the streets of the city run red with Trojan blood! Are you ready to give your life for Greece, Shermanus?"

This suddenly seemed like a horrible idea. "Sure thing, Mr. Agamemnon."

Once the Trojans let the wooden horse into their city, the Greek soldiers attacked. Swords clashed against shields and helmets. It was scary.

"**Aghh!**" I screamed. I reached inside my

uniform and pulled out the dog whistle Mr. Peabody had given me on the first day of school. I blew into it with all my might.

A moment later, Mr. Peabody swooped down and scooped me up. He kicked and blocked our way through the battle. "This is why I ask you to obey me, Sherman. I'm your father, and it's my job to keep you safe."

"But are you sure Miss Grunion won't take me away?" I asked.

"Not as long as I'm around," he replied. We made our way back to Penny in the Trojan horse.

Just as we reached the wooden horse, it started to roll toward a nearby cliff.

"Penny!" I shouted.

Mr. Peabody sprang onto a real horse that was nearby and pulled me up behind him. Using a rope, he lassoed the wooden horse to a stop on the cliff's edge. Then I held the rope tight so

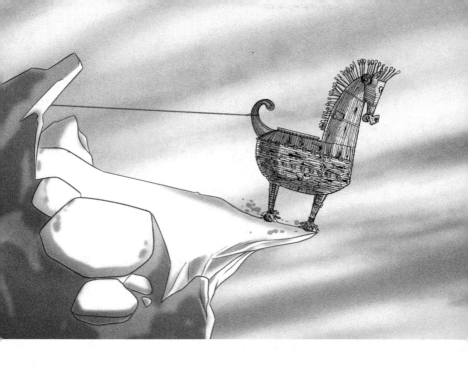

Mr. Peabody could zip-line down it to rescue Penny.

I jumped off to help and let go of the rope by mistake. **Uh-oh.**

The wooden horse slid toward the ravine—with all three of us inside!

Mr. Peabody jumped on a loose plank in the floor and catapulted Penny and me to safety. But he was still trapped!

The wooden horse toppled over the cliff, taking Mr. Peabody with it.

"Mr. Peabody!" I shouted. "What should I do?"

"There's nothing you can do, Sherman," Penny replied softly. "I just want to go home."

"Home?" Suddenly, I had an idea. "That's it! Come on!"

"Where are we going?" Penny asked. She struggling to keep up.

"We're going home," I replied, firing up the WABAC. "There's only one person who can help us, and that's Mr. Peabody."

"How is that even possible?" Penny asked, confused.

"We've got a time machine, Penny. I can set it so we'll get home when Mr. Peabody is still there."

Penny looked concerned. "But I thought

you're not supposed to go back to a time when you existed."

Penny had a point. But this was a special case. "What choice do we have?" I asked.

Just then, a red light on the WABAC's dash-board blinked.

"**ERROR!**" a robotic voice warned. "You are attempting to travel to an era in which you exist. This could alter the fabric of space-time. **ERROR!**"

I couldn't let my fear stop me. I smashed the override button. "Hang on!" I shouted.

Penny gripped her chair as the WABAC rocketed through the air.

Chapter 7

When we got home, Mr. Peabody was just where we'd left him—talking to Penny's parents. I had never been so happy to see him. We hid in the hallway and waved him over.

Mr. Peabody eyed our clothes. We were both dressed like ancient Greeks. "You used the WABAC!" he whispered.

"I did! I know!" I said. I tried to quickly explain everything we had been through. "And then you died in ancient Troy!" I finished. "But now you're here and everything's fine."

"Well, not exactly," Mr. Peabody said. He looked more worried than I had ever seen him. "I told you never to go back to a time when you

existed, because there'd be two of you."

"Yeah," I said, "but the other one of me is in ancient Egypt."

Just then, we heard the elevator ding. The doors opened, and another Sherman entered the room.

"Who are you?" I asked the Sherman from the past.

"He's you from another time," Mr. Peabody explained.

Past Sherman looked confused. "But I thought you said never to go back to a time when you existed."

"I know," I said. "But what was I supposed to do? Mr. Peabody died in ancient Troy."

"What are we going to do?" Penny asked. We were running out of time to set things right.

"Well, for starters," Mr. Peabody began, "both Shermans can't stay here."

I looked at Past Sherman. He seemed to be thinking the same thing I was: having a twin might be fun! We tried to high-five. But when our hands got close together, crackling energy zapped between our fingers. Ouch!

"See!" Mr. Peabody exclaimed. "We can't have two Shermans in the same time. It puts too much strain on the time-space continuum."

Mr. Peabody distracted the Petersons while Past Sherman dashed toward the elevator.

Ding! The doors opened again—and out stepped Miss Grunion!

"I've come for my inspection," she announced coldly.

"Of course. Why don't we start over here . . . or there?" Mr. Peabody suggested. He waved his hand back and forth, trying to hypnotize her. The Petersons started to fall into a trance again. So did Past Sherman! He crashed to the floor, waking up the Petersons.

"Sherman!" they exclaimed.

Miss Grunion looked from Past Sherman to me. "Wait! Is that . . ."

Before I could explain, the elevator opened once more.

Mr. Peabody strolled into the room dressed in Greek Army gear.

I ran toward him.

"You didn't die!" I cried happily.

"Of course I didn't die!" He explained how he'd made it back from the bottom of a Trojan ravine. Then he saw my double—and his.

"Sherman," he said seriously, "I've got to get you out of here before you touch yourself!"

"You're not going anywhere!" Miss Grunion declared. "I've seen quite enough to remove the boy—both boys—from this home."

"No!" Penny cried. "Please, Miss Grunion. This is my fault. I started it." She turned to me. "I'm sorry I picked on you, Sherman. I'm sorry I called you a dog."

"You have nothing to apologize for, Penny," Miss Grunion continued. "A dog should not have

been allowed to adopt a boy in the first place."
She grabbed Past Sherman and me by the arms.

We both tried to break free but accidentally
fell into each other.

"**Ahhh!**" we cried. We morphed into a knot of
cosmic energy. "Help!"

The two Peabodys rushed to pull us apart.
But it was too late. The lights flashed and the

ground shook. The four of us morphed into one giant ball of cosmic goo, then—**BOOM!**

After the explosion, there was just one me and one Mr. Peabody again.

Miss Grunion grabbed my arm. "I don't know what just happened here, but you are coming with me!" she ordered.

"Let me go!" I shouted.

Miss Grunion gripped me tighter.

"Ow! You're hurting me!" I cried.

At that, Mr. Peabody lunged forward. He bit Miss Grunion right on the arm!

I couldn't believe it.

"He bit me!" said Miss Grunion in shock. She took out her phone and dialed the police.

Mr. Peabody had only tried to protect me, but he had made things much worse.

"What are we going to do?" I asked.

"Run!" Mr. Peabody cried.

We sprinted for the WABAC. Penny followed close behind.

"I can't believe you bit her!" I said to Mr. Peabody.

"I know, Sherman. It was wrong," he replied.

"Wrong? It was **awesome**!"

We piled into the WABAC. Outside, we heard the Petersons, Miss Grunion, and the police shouting after us.

"And now to return to our proper time and erase this mess," Mr. Peabody said. He pushed a button.

The WABAC shot into the sky.

A moment later, an alarm sounded from the dash. "Time travel failed," the robotic voice warned.

"Oh, dear," Mr. Peabody sighed. "Our cosmic doubles colliding ripped a hole in the space-time continuum. That's why we can't get to the past."

Suddenly—**SPLAT!** Leonardo da Vinci smacked into our windshield, followed by King Tut!

I looked into the sky—it was raining historical figures! They were falling out of the hole.

"We need to get to the past," Mr. Peabody declared. He steered the WABAC through the air. Police helicopters followed.

"It looks like the past is coming to **us**!" I replied. I watched as Agamemnon fell through the sky.

"I'm trying to find another wormhole," Mr. Peabody said. He punched different dates into the computer, trying to find a way back in time. "But they all lead to the present!"

Outside the window, I saw a police helicopter heading right for us! "Look out!" I shouted.

Mr. Peabody slammed on the brakes. The WABAC dropped through the sky!

Chapter 8

The WABAC landed with a thud in a park. Outside, a crowd of people from the past ran toward it. I saw Agamemnon, da Vinci, and King Tut.

Then the police cars showed up. Miss Grunion stepped out of one.

"Come out, Peabody!" a policeman shouted into a megaphone. "You are under arrest!"

Mr. Peabody followed the officer's orders. "You don't understand," he began. "There's a rip in the space-time continuum. If you arrest me, I won't be able to fix it!"

"Take him away!" Miss Grunion commanded. A police officer put a collar around Mr. Peabody's neck.

"Wait!" I cried. "Mr. Peabody is the only one who can fix this problem. Please give him another chance! I'm the one who made all the mistakes. The only mistake Mr. Peabody ever made was . . . me."

"A *dog* should never have been allowed to adopt a *boy* in the first place!" Miss Grunion said.

Suddenly, I felt madder than I'd ever felt in my whole life. Miss Grunion didn't think Mr. Peabody was good for me—but I knew he was the best. He was my *dad*. "Maybe you're right, Miss Grunion. But there's one thing you haven't considered," I said.

"What's that?" she asked.

"I'm a dog, too," I stated.

"What?" She looked confused.

"If being a dog means you're like Mr. Peabody—who never turns his back on you, and loves you no matter how many times you mess up—then I'm a dog, too!" I shouted.

Mr. da Vinci stepped up next to me. "I'm a dog, too," he said.

The next thing I knew, Agamemnon, his army, King Tut—all of the people we'd met across space and time—stood by me and said the same thing. "I'm a dog, too." Even the Petersons joined in.

Penny put her arm around my shoulder. "I'm a dog, too," she added sweetly.

Miss Grunion frowned. "All right, fine; you're all dogs," she said. "But you can't change the law."

She was right. I couldn't change the law—but

I knew someone who could! George Washington stepped forward. "I hereby award Mr. Peabody a presidential pardon!" he announced. Mr. Peabody was free!

Miss Grunion really fumed. But I was too busy hugging Mr. Peabody to care.

• • •

A moment later, a whistling noise came from the wormhole above us. It took up half the sky now!

Mr. Peabody looked at all the famous faces before him. "This is the greatest collection of geniuses ever assembled. Surely we can come up with another way of getting to the past!"

Everyone started talking at once.

Then, suddenly, I had it! "I have an idea!" I shouted.

"What is it, Sherman?" Mr. Peabody asked, quieting the crowd.

"Why not go to the future?" I said. "I've never

been there before, so it's probably not as screwed up!"

"Sherman, that's it!" Mr. Peabody exclaimed. "If we set the WABAC for the future and go very fast . . . we'll create our own gravitational field . . . that's equal and opposite . . . to the rip in the time-space continuum!"

"I don't get it," Agamemnon said.

"We're going to fly up there and punch that big hole in the face!" I explained.

"Just a few seconds into the future should work," Mr. Peabody continued. "Then we will slingshot right back. Sherman, you're a genius."

I flashed a grin. "You hear that, Penny? I'm a genius."

Penny rolled her eyes. But she was smiling.

Mr. Peabody rushed into the WABAC. I followed, tripping up the steps. I might have been a genius, but I was still clumsy.

"I need to reprogram the WABAC," Mr. Peabody said. "That means *you* have to drive."

I could hardly believe my ears—Mr. Peabody had said I could drive the WABAC!

"In order to leap into the future, the WABAC will have to go faster than ever. Are you ready, Sherman?" Mr. Peabody asked.

"Ready!" I called.

Mr. Peabody punched some keys on the computer, programming the time machine.

"Now?" I asked.

"We need more speed!" Mr. Peabody shouted over the roar of the engine.

I pushed on the throttle. "Now?"

"Just a little more . . . ," Mr. Peabody told me. "Not yet, Sherman . . . not yet—**NOW!**"

I slammed my hand on a red button on the dash. **ZOOOOM!** We blasted through the wormhole into the future.

A few seconds later, the WABAC popped back into the calm blue sky above the park. We'd done it! The wormhole was gone—and so were all of our friends from the past. Agamemnon, Leonardo da Vinci, and everyone else had been sucked into the wormhole and returned to their places in history.

Penny and the Petersons waved to us from the ground. Penny told me later that Miss Grunion had been sucked into history with Agamemnon. I guess you could say our problems with her really were a thing of the past.

"**Woo-hoo!**" I cried.

Mr. Peabody and I high-fived.

"I love you, Sherman," Mr. Peabody said.

"I have a deep regard for you as well, Mr. Peabody," I replied. But really, I love him. He's my dad!

We're the perfect team. Just a dog and his boy who can handle anything together—past, present, or future!